# Dear Parents:

Congratulations! Your child is taking the first steps on an exciting journey. The destination? Independent reading!

**STEP INTO READING®** will help your child get there. The program offers five steps to reading success. Each step includes fun stories and colorful art or photographs. In addition to original fiction and books with favorite characters, there are Step into Reading Non-Fiction Readers, Phonics Readers and Boxed Sets, Sticker Readers, and Comic Readers—a complete literacy program with something to interest every child.

## Learning to Read, Step by Step!

### Ready to Read    Preschool–Kindergarten
• big type and easy words • rhyme and rhythm • picture clues
For children who know the alphabet and are eager to begin reading.

### Reading with Help    Preschool–Grade 1
• basic vocabulary • short sentences • simple stories
For children who recognize familiar words and sound out new words with help.

### Reading on Your Own    Grades 1–3
• engaging characters • easy-to-follow plots • popular topics
For children who are ready to read on their own.

### Reading Paragraphs    Grades 2–3
• challenging vocabulary • short paragraphs • exciting stories
For newly independent readers who read simple sentences with confidence.

### Ready for Chapters    Grades 2–4
• chapters • longer paragraphs • full-color art
For children who want to take the plunge into chapter books but still like colorful pictures.

**STEP INTO READING®** is designed to give every child a successful reading experience. The grade levels are only guides; children will progress through the steps at their own speed, developing confidence in their reading.

Remember, a lifetime love of reading starts with a single step!

Step into Reading, Random House, and the Random House colophon are registered trademarks of Penguin Random House LLC.

Visit us on the Web!
StepIntoReading.com
rhcbooks.com

Educators and librarians, for a variety of teaching tools, visit us at
RHTeachersLibrarians.com

ISBN 978-0-593-12134-4 (trade) — ISBN 978-0-593-12135-1 (lib. bdg.)

Printed in the United States of America

10 9 8 7 6 5 4 3 2 1

# MIGHTY TWINS!

by Tex Huntley

based on the teleplay
"Pups Meet the Mighty Twins"
by Andy Guerdat and Steve Sullivan

illustrated by MJ Illustrations

Random House 🏠 New York

Shake!

Shake!

Shake!

The Adventure Bay Bridge
is falling down!

Ryder and the Mighty Pups
are on the roll!

Two new pups

want to help.

# They are twins!

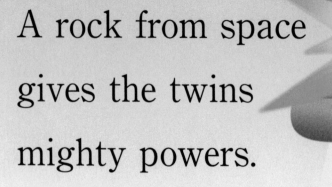

A rock from space
gives the twins
mighty powers.

Now they are the
Mighty Twins!

One pup can
grow big!

One pup can
become small!

The twins help
the Mighty Pups.

They will save
the bridge!

The big pup
holds up the bridge.

The small pup
works with Rubble.

# The twins helped
# save the day!

They are now
part of the
PAW Patrol.

They even get
their own car!

# Hooray for the Mighty Pups!